D0416764

About the author

Jean Murray has found her passion in writing in her mid 40s. She takes delight in sharing the knowledge that when you believe in something that you can do and if you work really hard on it then the outcome will be successful.

Dedication

Dedicated to Joey Hanway and his dog Patch
Also my Dad Christy who plays the granddad in the story.

Jean Murray

MADHEAD THE CRAZY HORSE

AUSTIN MACAULEY
PUBLISHERS LTD.

Copyright © Jean Murray (2015)

The right of Jean Murray to be identified as author of this work has been asserted by her in accordance with section 77 and 78 of the Copyright, Designs and Patents Act 1988.

All rights reserved. No part of this publication may be reproduced, stored in a retrieval system, or transmitted in any form or by any means, electronic, mechanical, photocopying, recording, or otherwise, without the prior permission of the publishers.

Any person who commits any unauthorized act in relation to this publication may be liable to criminal prosecution and civil claims for damages.

A CIP catalogue record for this title is available from the British Library.

ISBN 9781785549557 (Paperback)
ISBN 9781785549564 (Hardback)

www.austinmacauley.com

First Published (2015)
Austin Macauley Publishers Ltd.
25 Canada Square
Canary Wharf
London
E14 5LQ

Printed and bound in Great Britain

Acknowledgments

I would like to acknowledge the creator of Madhead, my husband Anthony. For Yasmin, who kept him funny and rude!

Thank you Sarah for your beautiful drawings.

Thank you to Brian Duff for allowing Broad Meadows Stables to be used in my story and for giving myself and my girls the wonderful experiences of horses. Thanks to Anna and Sarah and Connie and Simone for inspiring all of the children to compete in challenging competitions. For Sandra, who manages the shows and lessons and distributes countless rosettes! Thanks to all the many teachers at Broad Meadows that have taught Yasmin how to jump! Keith, Barbara, Michelle and Caroline. Thanks to Hazel O'Flynn, another great teacher to Sarah when she was on ponies. To Colette who keeps all the parents fed in the coffee shop. Thanks to all the mammy's who support our children's love of horses, by mucking out, feeding and putting the beloved ponies out to the paddocks every day and for the many reassuring hugs from all the mammies who support each other through tears and falls.

A special thanks to all of Yasmin's friends at Broad Meadows Stables, Rachael, Libby, Hannah, Grace, Aoife, Ami Hugs, Kate, Robyn, Alanna, Aoife R, Mia, Andrea, Amie H, little Ami, Margaret, Chloe, Tiana, Sadbh and Blaithin for their beautiful personalities.

Thank you to Helen Mortimer, Sarah's art teacher in Ratoath College secondary school who inspired Sarah's dedication to illustration and continues to inspire the future artists to come.

To IADT College in Dun Laoghaire and its dedicated tutors for providing an excellence in Art education.'

For the memory of Julie Whelan who sadly passed during the production of this book'

Chapter 1

Broad Meadows Stables is a beautiful livery yard stretching over acres of lush green fields in the middle of County Meath. The land is full of beautiful mares and stallions running free with their foals. Twin boys, David and Gary Kelly, age 30, own the stables. It was left to them by their beloved father, whose passion was breeding horses. The two young men are as different as chalk and cheese. Gary loves the dangers of galloping across country and is quite fearless, whereas David likes to keep his feet on the ground in dressage. David is mean and moody to the children and the horses and Gary is a happy chap and loves everyone and every animal.

Broad Meadows Stables is a very popular yard for riding lessons; it attracts lots of children and adults from different areas in Meath and there are plenty of lessons to suit everybody's level of experience. It has loads of stables for the large selection of horses and ponies liveried at the yard and a huge indoor arena where everybody runs to in the regular downpours of Irish rain. Madhead is one of the ponies at Broad Meadows. He is a six years old brown and white cob. None of the children ever want to ride Madhead because he always manages to throw them off. He doesn't like jumping and he doesn't like trotting.

Gary is always trying to convince the braver girls to ride him; "Look at him girls, he's really cute don't you think? He's got those cute little fluffy white feathers at the bottom of his legs. He's really quite handsome!"

The girls looked over at Madhead, with his square oblong head neighing, his lips parted in a 'dare me' smile, showing a big, wide set of teeth.

He then proceeded to spread his legs wide and do a gigantic wee.

"I don't know, he looks a bit vicious!" one of the young girls replied as the others ran off in case they were asked to ride the crazy horse.

"Poor Madhead! Nobody gets you, do they fella?" Gary rubbed Madhead's nose. "Your just full of fun, that's all, there's not a vicious bone in you!"

Gary was worried about what would become of Madhead. The truth was that Madhead was very rude and very naughty. The other ponies at the yard wouldn't even ride beside him during the lessons.

"At least he has you Betsy," Gary reached over to brush the bay mare's mane. Betsy nuzzled Madhead in response. At eight years old, Betsy was like a big sister to Madhead. She's tried many times to keep Madhead out of trouble, but sometimes she can't prevent him from jumping over the fences in the field and causing chaos at their stables.

One busy Saturday morning at Broad Meadows, the ponies were getting tacked up for the lessons. The children arrived early to check the list to see which pony they were assigned to. Madhead could hear the shouts of joy when each child got any pony but him.

Madhead was upset because nobody wanted him, but it was easier to pretend that he didn't want anyone riding him, so he behaved really badly. He wouldn't let the groom tack him up. Madhead was snorting and holding his ears back and kicking at the other ponies. Pretty soon, the yard had turned into chaos. The children were crying and all the ponies were stamping their hooves!

"That frigging pony!" David said to himself. "I'm getting rid of that crazy horse if it's the last thing I'll do!"

But, as usual, his nicer brother Gary soothed things over with ease. "Come on now kids, why don't you all come down and meet the new baby foals that have just arrived last night!"

All the kids wiped their eyes and eagerly followed Gary to see the new babies.

Madhead had finally calmed down and when his door was left open by accident, he bolted from the stable. He galloped all over the yard, only stopping to rear up on his hind legs.

"Oh Madhead!" Betsy said as she raced after him. Betsy knew that Madhead was feeling sad because nobody wanted to ride him. Why couldn't they see that Madhead was really a nice pony? David chased after the two naughty ponies, silently forming his plan in his head.

The next morning was Monday, the 1st day of September. Monday is always a very quiet day at Broad Meadows Stables as everyone has a day off, even the ponies and horses. David is the only person that works on Mondays. He normally feeds the horses

4

and turns them out to the field. Having nobody around also gave him the opportunity that he needed that morning, to carry out his evil plan. David was finally going to get rid of that crazy horse Madhead!

He found a perfect place for him that no one would find him ever again.

Madhead didn't like David very much. He watched with interest as David reversed a horse box into the yard.

"What's he up to?" wondered Madhead as he munched his hay. David then came and put Madhead's head collar on and loaded him into the box. David looked in at Betsy. "I'd better take you with him, you're almost as much trouble!"

David quickly loaded Betsy into the horsebox too. He secured them in and quickly drove off.

"Oh Madhead, what's going on? Where are we going?" Betsy asked Madhead worriedly.

David drove for a while. Madhead and Betsy had never been outside Broad Meadows before and they didn't know what was going on. They were getting a bit uneasy when David finally came to a stop. He came around to the back of the horsebox and let the ponies out into a small field, laden with rubbish. The ponies looked around them. They looked at David worriedly, but David had no sympathy.

"Ha Ha! Good riddance to you both, especially you Madhead, you crazy horse!" David laughed wickedly.

He then got back in the truck and just drove off without them. The ponies were left confused and hungry. There was a canal and there was a train track but there were no stables.

"Oh dear me!" said Betsy, "You've really done it this time!"

Madhead was full of guilt. Now his silly behaviour had affected his friend.

David was working his plan in his head as he drove back to Broad Meadows. He couldn't believe how easy it was. He should've got rid of that Madhead a long time ago. He'd tell Gary that the two ponies had gotten very bad colic in the night and he had to put them out of their misery. Gary would never know!

"Yes! I've done it!" The mean old brother laughed happily to himself as he drove back with the empty horsebox.

Chapter 2

Madhead and Betsy had no choice but to try settle in at this new place. They had thought about trying to get back home, but they didn't know where home was. There was a little bit of shelter under the bridge and they stayed there when it rained heavily. They were often hungry as there was less and less grass each day. They also missed their old stables and all the children. It was such a happy yard. They missed their owner Gary so much.

Meanwhile, back at Broad Meadows Stables, closer than they knew, Gary was heartbroken over the loss of his beloved ponies.

"Of course, my brother David had no choice but to put them down. Colic is an awful thing for a pony to get. It causes severe pain and it could take hours of agonizing pain to die..." Gary reassured himself. "It was so good of David to have their bodies taken care of also. That was very considerate of him."

Gary didn't realize that David hated his ponies.

A few weeks later, on a cold damp day in October, a kind old man spotted the ponies beside the canal. He had a big smiley face with silver white hair. His tanned scalp shone on the top of his bald head. He brought Madhead and Betsy some hay and oats. The old man assumed someone already owned the ponies but decided to bring them a treat anyway. He was surprised to see that they were quite neglected.

He said, "You poor old devils, you're half starved!"

The old man checked their hooves and teeth and felt their bones jutting from their shabby coats.

"I guess I came just in the nick of time with these oats!"

The ponies neighed in delight at the sight of the oats. They began to eat hungrily. He rubbed them tenderly as he spoke to them.

"What do you call yourselves?" He asked as he checked their head collars. "You can call me Joey and this is my dog Patch."

The two ponies looked at the tiny little dog and neighed loudly as they nuzzled him. Joey looked at them and knew they were happy to be found. The cob had a big square head with one blue eye and one brown eye. His mouth was really wide, like he was grinning all the time.

"You're a strange looking fella, with that big head on you! Madhead is a good name for you!" Joey said.

Madhead chuckled. He looked at the bay pony. "You're quite a strong lady, aren't you now? Betsy suits you well," he said as he patted her coat.

She neighed her response happily, nuzzling him in the neck. They were going to be best friends. Joey took some grooming tools from his pouch. He began to comb their tangled manes and tails and brushed their coats till they gleamed. He took their old shoes off and clipped their hooves.

9

"You won't need shoes in the field now," Joey said to Madhead's questioning face.

A few hours later and Madhead and Betsy felt much better, just like their old selves.

"There now, Madhead and Betsy," Joey said admiringly. "I'm off home now, but I'll be back tomorrow with some more food. Come on Patch!" he called as he walked away with his little Jack Russell, who skipped faithfully beside him.

"Thank goodness that nice old man found us! Isn't he so nice? He has such a smiley face too!"

Betsy swooned gratefully, as she looked at the old man walk away. .

"He came just in time too!" Madhead replied. "I haven't had a proper pooh in ages. These oats will help me a lot!"

He lifted his tail and let it go... and go... and go... and go... and go... and finally...

"Ahhhhh! That felt so good! Can you smell that Betsy?" he asked in delight as he galloped off.

"Catch me if you can!" Betsy looked at huge pile of pooh on the ground.

"Ugh! You're soooo disgusting!" she shouted after him, laughing as she tried to catch him.

Chapter 3

Madhead and Betsy chased each other around happily. Madhead had always dreamed of being a show jumper in his last home, but he just couldn't jump. He seemed to fall over his feet and the saddle always seemed to hurt too. He never knew why the kids seemed scared of him.

"Ah, maybe it wasn't meant to be?" he reassured himself. Now, he had loads of time to jump the piles of rubbish in the field and it seemed to be getting easier. The two ponies stopped to look at a rattling train going by on the old tracks on the bridge.

It was unusual, as trains never came by this way anymore. It was a small trailer train but it was going really fast. Madhead and Betsy watched with great interest, it was making a lot of noise.

Suddenly! There was an awful screeching sound. It seemed to be trying to slow down coming down a slope. Madhead and Betsy's ears went back in fright! The train had come off the tracks, tumbling and crashing down the hill as it went. It took ages to stop. Finally, all went quiet when the bashed up train landed upside down at the edge of the canal. Madhead and Betsy looked at the carnage curiously.

"Do you think there's anything in there?" Betsy asked Madhead.

"There could be oats and hay!" Madhead answered. "That'd be so cool!"

"Is that all you ever think about Madhead?" she asked him.

"No! I think of farting and poohing too!" he giggled.

"There could be somebody hurt!" Betsy said worriedly.

As they went towards the wreck, they heard a cough and a splutter. Through the dust, a beautiful grey pony appeared. She was a petite little thing, but she looked beautifully groomed and her mane and tail were plaited perfectly.

Madhead trotted over to have a better look. He hadn't noticed the oil in the mud and his two front legs slipped and went flat out in front of him, followed quickly by his two hind legs!

"Aghhh!" He screamed as he skidded all the way over and landed on top of the little pony, knocking her straight down into the mud!

"Ooops!" Madhead said, looking directly into the pony's beautiful blue eyes. "How ya?" he said, "I'm Madhead and this is Betsy." '

He nodded towards his friend who was laughing her head off. "Let me help you up?"

Madhead put his head under the little pony's chest to try lift her out of the mud. His bottom was very close to her face when a big fart escaped him!

"Ughh! You're soooo disgusting!" said Betsy and the little pony at the same time. The two girls giggled.

"Are you ok?" Betsy asked the little pony as she observed the damage. "That was a pretty bad crash you have just walked out of!"

The little pony was trying to shake some of the wet mud off her.

"Maybe you should rest for a moment, what's your name?" Betsy said as she tried to rub off some of the mud.

"I'm.... I don't know my name, but I think I'm ok."

The little pony looked around her. She had no idea where she was. "I'm just covered in muck!"

"Mmm, yes, you are a bit!" Betsy said as she glared at Madhead, but Betsy was concerned about the little pony. She may have banged her head in the crash and lost her memory. She thought some cold water would bring it back. "But don't worry, a little dip in the canal will have you all clean again!"

The pony looked over at the canal. "No way! I'm not going in there!" she protested as Madhead happily grabbed the lead rope attached to her and pulled her towards the canal.

"Oh, oh, oh, it's freezing!" she cried as she landed in the muddy water.

Madhead was jumping about making an awful splash. "Ahhhh!" the little pony screamed angrily.

Madhead had never seen a female pony so annoyed before. He was getting a bit worried. When Madhead starts to worry, he starts to belch. Great big thunderous belches! He let out a little belch, then a big belch, then a bigger belch!

"B...EE...LL...CHHH!"

The pony stopped crying and looked at him quizzically. His face was all puffed, his eyes were bulging, his lips were swollen from trying to hold his mouth closed to stop the biggest bellowing belch escape…

It didn't work and out came BEL! BELC! BELCHHHUROOOOORH! It was the loudest, rudest belch she had ever heard!

"Wow! That was a crazy sound!" she said, amazed, her tears finally stopping. Madhead noticed her name was on her head collar.

"Hey! Your name is Cleo! Come on Cleo, jump around, you'll soon warm up," Madhead said with a big grin on his face.

"Cleo doesn't really sound like my name," she thought. "How strange?" She started to jump around in the water anyway. It was fun! She ran and splashed a bit more and was soon giggling happily. It felt kind of good actually.

Madhead felt relieved; he didn't like being worried. He much preferred laughing, after poohing and farting that is!

Betsy wasn't going to miss out on the fun. She jumped right in beside them. They played happily for hours. They had completely forgotten that there was a driver of the train and he was nowhere to be seen!

Chapter 4

The next morning as the three ponies were scratching their dried muddy backs against the trees, they saw Joey, the old man, coming across the lock on the canal. They galloped over to him neighing good morning.

"Hey, I'm glad to see you ponies too!" Joey gave them a little cuddle and a carrot each. "Who have we here then? Where did you come from?" Joey asked the little pony. "Ok, ok, I'll give you a carrot too!" he said kindly to her as she was shyly nudging his pouch.

The little pony had a head collar on her and he could see the name engraved was Cleo.

"Hello Cleo!" he said as he patted her neck. "You're a scruffy lot today! What were you all up too? It'll take me all morning to clean you up!"

Joey had a box with him that caught the ponies' attention.

Madhead and Betsy were nudging the square box with their noses, while Cleo was chewing on her carrot. Joey pressed a button on the box and the two ponies jumped back as a big loud noise escaped. "That's called a CD player." Joey told their startled faces. That's Mario Lanza singing. It's called Opera."

Madhead looked at Cleo, she seemed to love the music.

"Have you heard that before?" he asked her.

"I don't know, I can't remember anything!" she said worriedly.

"That Mario fella is rather good!" Betsy said as she listened to the loud tones of Mario blasting into the wind as Joey brushed her mane.

Madhead farted loudly in response!

When they were all groomed and fed, Joey took a walk down towards the bridge. He was wondering where Cleo had come from. Beneath the caked in mud on Cleo, Joey discovered a very pretty pony. He knew she was well looked after.

Betsy, Cleo and Madhead walked behind him, Madhead nipping and biting at the two girls in devilment all the way. "Come on Madhead, stop messing about, you devil!" Joey spoke kindly. Madhead snorted in answer.

Joey sped up as he noticed the broken up train on the tracks. He was amazed that Cleo had survived that wreckage. He also noticed the huge oil spill which must have caused the derailment. Joey could tell it wasn't a passenger train and there weren't any more ponies inside. So he looked around for the driver.

"Whoever it is, his chances of surviving this don't look good!" he said to the worried looking ponies.

"How did we not realize there was someone driving the train? I feel so awful knowing someone was here alone all night!" said Betsy.

There wasn't much left of the drivers cab, it was quite bashed up. The carnage was everywhere. Joey searched the wreck, but he couldn't see the train driver anywhere. Finally, he heard a weak voice calling…

"Help, help!"

Joey pulled at the wreckage, lifting as much debris as he could. He could see the driver! He was alive! Joey tried to lift the wreckage up but it was too heavy. He had to go for help.

"Stay here gang, I'll be back as quick as I can." The three ponies stayed beside the train driver and nuzzled his face in comfort.

After what seemed like ages, Joey came back with two firemen and two ambulance men, who carried a stretcher. The firemen had to use a lot of electric cutting tools to be able to remove the heaviest pieces. The ponies stood close by, watching with interest.

At last the firemen were able to lift the rest of the wreckage up off the train driver. The ambulance men were then able to examine the train driver. There was blood on his head and he seemed to be unconscious. His leg was also sticking out at a funny angle. They put some bandages on his head and a big plastic bag on his leg. They then put a needle in his arm and attached it to a bag full of fluid. At last they declared they were ready to take him to hospital.

"Thanks to you Joey, the train driver is going to be just fine. It looks like he has a sore head and a broken leg, but it can be fixed," the ambulance man reassured him. The ponies were delighted. They didn't like to see anyone hurt.

"Well, that was a grand bit of excitement now, wasn't it?" Joey said to the ponies.

Joey had no idea that Cleo had lost her memory and that she didn't recognize the train driver. She still couldn't remember who she was or where she came from. It was a mystery.

"Did you recognize him Cleo?" Madhead asked her.

He thought it was cool to lose your memory. He'd love that to happen to him.

"No, I didn't! This is getting a bit scary," she replied.

"Don't worry Cleo, your memory will come back soon," Betsy reassured her.

Joey took his hatchet from his pouch. "There's no fixing this carriage now, no point in wasting the wood. It'll make a grand bit of firewood!"

As Joey chopped the wood, the ponies galloped around in delight.

Madhead was bored already. "Catch me if you can!" he challenged her as he kicked mud in her face. "Come on Betsy! Cleo's on!"

Chapter 5

The weeks went by and day after day, Joey came to look after the ponies. Cleo still couldn't remember who she was but she was happy with her new friends. Joey brought his wheelbarrow with him and chopped up the carriage for hours each day. He lit a bonfire every day with the scraps of wood and they all huddled round it on the really cold days. There was soon nothing left but the trailer.

"This'll come in handy too, no point leaving it to rot!" he said to Patch.

Joey loved collecting all sorts of things. His garage was full of old junk. He would find some use for the old trailer.

Patch began to bark at someone coming down the hill. It was a little girl followed by a man walking on crutches. Cleo remembered the voice! It was Yasmin's voice! Cleo neighed in excitement.

"Cleo! Cleo!" shouted the little girl happily as she hugged her pony. "I've missed you so much! I thought I'd never see you again!"

Cleo galloped over to her friends Betsy and Madhead.

"That's Yasmin! I remember! And her Granddad Christy! He's the train driver! They've come back for me!" she told them excitedly. "This is great, I'm going home at last!" Betsy was delighted that Cleo's memory returned. It must have been the shock of hearing her owner's voice.

"I knew it would come back!" She nuzzled Cleo.

Yasmin's Granddad Christy was thanking Joey for looking after Cleo. He wasn't very old at 64 and had been a train driver all his life. He explained how he had crashed. He told Joey that he had been taking Cleo to get a special saddle made. He had brought her in the small carriage train while he was doing a delivery in the same area. He thought it would be quicker to use the old track but hadn't realized it wasn't safe. He wasn't sure that Cleo had survived the crash at all. He was so grateful to joey.

Madhead was nuzzling Cleo too. He was going to miss her. Joey, Yasmin and Christy were watching the ponies neighing and frolicking with each other.

"Look Granddad!" Yasmin said; "Doesn't that pony look just like Madhead the pony, from your friend Gary's yard?"

Yasmin's Granddad looked at Madhead cuddling Cleo. "Yes he does! I'd swear it was the same pony, only Gary said he had died of colic, and the mare Betsy too. Poor old Gary misses those ponies so much."

"That's funny," Joey piped in, "Their head collars were engraved with the names Madhead and Betsy!"

"Oh Goodness! I bet Gary's mean brother David had something to do with this! He hated Madhead! Wait until I tell Gary that his beloved ponies are alive and looking better than ever!" Christy said delightedly.

It was time to go. Christy put the lead rope on Cleo. He shook Joey's hand in thanks.

"I'll give Gary the news about Madhead and Betsy, I'm sure he'll be really happy that they are safe and well."

Joey gave Cleo a pat on the back. "Good luck girl!"

He was sad to think that all the ponies would be gone from him soon. Betsy and Madhead stood beside Joey and neighed their goodbyes.

Cleo was too excited to notice that Madhead was sad at the thought of not seeing her again.

"Goodbye!" she called as she got in her box and was driven back to her home.

Chapter 6

The days passed sadly for Madhead. He couldn't eat much and he wasn't interested in Betsy or Patch's chasing games. He didn't even laugh when Betsy made lots of attempts at ice skating across the canal only to land on her bottom every time! It was almost Christmas and the snow was heavy on the ground. Joey was planning some lovely treats to try and cheer Madhead up. Gary hadn't come for the ponies yet, so Joey was still happy to take care of them. He loved their company.

Cleo had been back at her own stables for two weeks now. She was nice and cosy in her warm rugs and heated stables, but she was off her food too. She couldn't believe that she was missing that crazy pony Madhead and the lovable Betsy! She missed Joey and Patch too. She was so confused. She loved Yasmin so much too.

As promised, Christy had gone over to Broad Meadows to see Gary. He found him as usual in the field with the ponies.

"Hi there Christy! How are you healing after your crash?"

Gary gave his pal a warm hug.

"I'm doing just great, thanks Gary, but I've got some news for you."

Christy told him that he had found Madhead and Betsy abandoned by the crash site, but that they were ok.

A nice old man had been looking after them. Gary was shocked. He was so annoyed at his brother. He couldn't believe that David would do something like this to him. He had to get him back. He thanked Christy and said he needed to go off and think of a plan to get even on his brother!

"Oh dear," thought Christy. "Brothers!"

Yasmin was brushing down Cleo's coat when her granddad came back.

"Cleo hasn't been her usual self since we brought her home. Do you think she misses her friends?"

"I think so pet. She seems to be fretting," replied her granddad.

"Should we bring Cleo back to Madhead and Betsy?" Yasmin asked him.

Cleo's ears perked up. She nuzzled Yasmin.

"I think she's given you her answer!" Yasmin's granddad smiled.

"Let's get her ready then!" Yasmin hugged her granddad and Cleo.

Chapter 7

"I have it!" Gary sniggered to himself, as he began to put his plan in action. He knew his brother David was scared of the horses,, so he was going to pretend that Madhead and Betsy's ghosts had come back to haunt him.

He got some help from the kids in the yard, who were happy to help him. They thought David was really mean! The kids were really good on their iPod things. They were able to create lots of different special effects with the latest technology. They had gone into the attic earlier in the day to set up their equipment. They drilled little holes into his bedroom ceiling so that they could project their images.

"Well done kids, this is going to scare the living daylights out of him!" Gary said delightedly.

They began that night. After David was sound asleep, the kids turned a stereo sound of galloping hooves and wind blowing and neighing. Through the holes, they projected Madhead and Betsy's image onto the walls. They had to hold their laughter in as David began to shake in the bed as he pulled the covers right over him, "Go away! Go away!" he whimpered.

The next day, Gary pretended he knew nothing as David walked around looking like a zombie. Gary chuckled to himself. It took only two more nights before David came running into Gary's bedroom.

"It was me! I left those poor old ponies beside that old train track to die and now they've come back to haunt me!" David wailed. "I'm so sorry! How can I ever make it up to you?' He was filled with guilt.

Gary laughed hard and all the kids came running in behind David laughing their heads off. "What's all this?" David asked. "Christy told me of your wicked deed, I had to get you back! And don't worry, I'll think of some way you can make it up to me." Gary said smugly.

Chapter 8

It was Christmas Eve at last. Joey had come back from helping out at the dog pound, his other passion. He put more wood on his bonfire and took out some carrots and apples for the ponies and a nice bone for Patch. The sky was clear and crisp. The snow was hard on the ground. He sat beside the bonfire and opened a flask of hot turkey soup. He played his Christmas songs on his cd player and Madhead came over and nuzzled him. Betsy came over and nuzzled Madhead. This was her family. She was very grateful for this lovely night.

They all looked up together when they heard a truck come down the hill, followed by a jeep.

Madhead leaped up with joy when he saw Cleo's head poking out. He ran over towards it.

"Hi guys!" Cleo called as she came out of her trailer. "I couldn't stay away. I missed you all too much!"

"Yeah! We missed you too!" Madhead nuzzled her happily while Betsy watched a man get out of the jeep.

"Gary!" She trotted over to him.

"Hello girl, you didn't think I'd forget all about you now, did you?" Gary hugged her. "Or you

Madhead?" Gary gave Madhead a good pat on the back.

Betsy, Cleo and Madhead were so happy that they all galloped around in the snow. Patch was running round and round chasing his tail. He was so happy too!

"Merry Christmas!" Yasmin said to Joey as she hugged him. Christy had introduced Gary to Joey and they were shaking hands.

"Gary, did you tell Joey your plan? Can I tell him please, please?" Yasmin squealed excitedly.

"Go on then," said Gary, happy to let everyone know the good news.

"Gary is building a small stables right here, so that Madhead and Betsy and Cleo can stay together! And so that you can look after them! And I can help! Can I help? Please?" Yasmin blurted out quickly in case she forgot a word.

"Goodness, that's great news altogether! Of course I'll look after them and of course you can help little Yasmin! Merry Christmas!" Joey shook Christy's hand and Gary's hand again with a big smile on his face. "Come over to the fire now and have some turkey soup!"

Chapter 9

Madhead was so happy! He started to belch! He couldn't help it. He belched louder and louder. Yasmin started to laugh. She had never heard a horse belch before. She laughed so much, she got the hiccups!

"What a rude pony!" She hiccupped. Madhead, Betsy and Cleo neighed with laughter.

Madhead's mouth widened into a big grin.

"What does Cleo see in you?" Yasmin asked fondly as she rubbed Madhead's nose. Joey, Christy and Gary laughed out loud!

Chapter 10

So that was how the three ponies became firm friends and the new stables was called The Railer. In the years that followed, people would stop on the bridge and watch the goings on of the stables below. They watched lots of children taking their riding lessons and they heard plenty of laughter. They loved to watch the young girl with the strawberry colored hair jump the various courses with ease on her beloved ponies. Madhead had learned to wear a saddle and he had learned to jump the courses. He also competed in other competitions around the country and he was winning lots of rosettes. When the lessons were finished for the evening, people on the bridge would watch the old man and the little girl grooming and feeding their ponies together, chatting and laughing happily.

A while after that, they saw the young girl feeding and grooming while chatting to the kind old man sitting on a log with the little dog Patch by his side.

Epilogue

Today, a young woman called Yasmin takes care of the stables and her beloved old ponies.

She teaches the children to ride. People smile at the sight of the young woman chatting to the ponies and them neighing in response, with the little dog Patch by her side.

As for David, Gary's mean old twin brother, he has spent lots of years cleaning out stables and shoveling horse pooh, but not in the dark.

He's scared of the dark!